FRIEND OR FOE?

Adapted by Matthew J. Gilbert

Based on the teleplays
"Enemy of My Enemy" by Kenny Byerly and
"Karai's Vendetta" by Russ Carney and Ron Corcillo

RANDOM HOUSE  NEW YORK

Published in the United States by Random House Children's Books, a
division of Random House LLC, 1745 Broadway, New York, NY 10019,
and in Canada by Random House of Canada Limited, Toronto, Penguin
Random House Companies. Random House and the colophon are
registered trademarks of Random House LLC. Nickelodeon, Teenage
Mutant Ninja Turtles, and all related titles, logos, and characters are
trademarks of Viacom International Inc. and Viacom Overseas Holdings
C.V. Based on characters created by Peter Laird and Kevin Eastman.

randomhouse.com/kids

ISBN 978-0-385-38505-3

Printed in the United States of America
10 9 8 7 6 5 4 3 2 1

TEENAGE MUTANT NINJA TURTLES

FRIEND OR FOE?

High above the quiet, shadowy streets, the Teenage Mutant Ninja Turtles—Leonardo, Donatello, Raphael, and Michelangelo—stood watch over New York City on their nightly patrol. Normally, the ninja brothers would be scanning the streets below for any signs of crime.

But not tonight.

Tonight, their eyes were on the skies. Leo looked through his long-range spyglass at the skyline. He focused his lens on a facility a few blocks away that seemed to be haloed by a spooky pink glow: the Techno Cosmic Research Institute, otherwise known as T.C.R.I.

After weeks of observation, the Turtles knew

this was the secret headquarters of the Kraang—extra-dimensional aliens that were hiding on Earth and planning something big. But *what?*

Leo broke the silence to give his report to the others. "Nothing happening at T.C.R.I.—"

"Yet!" Donnie added in a skeptical tone. A few days earlier, the Turtles had discovered a secret Kraang storage device that contained a detailed file on their best friend—and Donnie's dream girl—April O'Neil. So it was no big surprise that his nerves were somewhat on edge now.

The same could not be said for Mikey. He was completely at ease, playing video games on his T-Phone.

"This game is awesome!" he exclaimed, mashing buttons. "The combat is so realistic."

"You want me to make it *more* realistic?" Raph threatened, cracking his knuckles at him.

"Guys!" Leo piped up, taking charge. "Stop messing around!"

Donnie punched in a few commands on his T-Phone's decoder app while he addressed his brothers. "According to the Kraang storage device that I decrypted, some kind of scouting ship is coming through the Kraang Portal tonight."

Leo glared at Mikey, who was still nose-deep in his game.

"So we all have to . . . STAY ALERT," Leo said to Mikey even more loudly.

"Yeah, you never know what could sneak up on you," said a soft voice from the dark.

Before the Turtles could react, a graceful figure somersaulted off a nearby water tower and onto the rooftop.

It was Karai, Shredder's beautiful teenage ninja soldier.

Leo locked eyes with her, remembering the last time he'd seen her: It was in a secret Kraang lab. She'd double-crossed them, trapping them inside with a grotesque super-mutant code named

'Justin,' a monstrosity made up of every kind of animal DNA known to man. The Turtles had only narrowly escaped its clutches.

"Cute, Karai, but I'm not in the mood," Leo told her.

He didn't want to admit it, but just seeing her stirred up a lot of old feelings. She might have sworn her allegiance to their archenemy, but he couldn't help admiring her skills.

Ignoring his words, Karai drew her *katana* and charged at Leo. Their blades clashed immediately. Leo expertly fended off her attacks. With one swift move, he swung both his blades and knocked her back.

"We don't have time for this!" Leo insisted. "Guys!"

On cue, Mikey yelled, *"Booyakasha!"* and the rest of the Turtles charged into battle.

Karai darted back and forth, acrobatically dodging each blow.

"Booyakasha?" she asked, landing with catlike finesse. "What does that even mean?"

"I don't know," Mikey replied innocently. "But it's fun to yell!"

And with that, Mikey surprised Karai with his secret throwing chain. She tumbled back, but recovered quickly. Showing off her ninja prowess, she made quick work of Donnie, Raph, and Mikey. It wasn't long before she locked blades with Leo again and they were face to face.

"You really know how to make a girl feel welcome," Karai taunted, putting Leo on the defensive. "I heard the scrawny one mention the Kraang. What's going on?"

Leo lunged forward. "None of your business—"

"And I'm not scrawny," Donnie interrupted them. "I'm *svelte.*"

Karai refused to back down. "Oh, c'mon! Let me in on the fun!"

Raph had had enough of this. He stepped forward and tried to talk some sense into her. "Look, we're a little busy trying to stop an alien invasion here, so do us a favor and get lost!"

Karai paused, lowering her sword. "An alien

invasion? Are you serious?" she asked with concern.

Suddenly, the roof began to rumble. The entire city seemed to be shaking. They all looked up to see the T.C.R.I. rooftop open like an aircraft hangar. Within seconds, a saucer-shaped Kraang ship with flowing tentacle sensors floated out of it.

"This can't be good," Leo whispered.

The Turtles and Karai were frozen. The sight of an extraterrestrial scout ship flying over New York scared them all speechless.

Finally, Mikey spoke. "Ummm, guys . . . I think I need to change my shell."

CHAPTER 2

Inside the scout ship, two blobby Kraang sat at the helm of a mobile alien command center. All around them, monitors and control panels flashed and oozed light. With the click of a button, a sophisticated radar screen began mapping the rooftops for any sign of movement. The system quickly zeroed in on five living, breathing targets.

One Kraang turned to the other and droned, "The ones who are called Turtles have been detected by the scanner which scans for Turtles."

"They are knowing too much of Kraang's plan," the other Kraang announced. "Attack."

The ship cut through the atmosphere, nose-diving toward Karai and the Turtles.

"I hope you have a plan for fighting that thing," Karai told Leo.

"Of course I do," Leo said. And then he turned back to her and hastily added, "Step one . . . run!"

They sprinted for their lives as the scout ship laser-blasted the rooftop to rubble. Leo led the way through the dust cloud, diving to the city streets below. Karai and the other Turtles followed, bouncing off rickety fire escapes and landing painfully on the pavement. They all scurried to the safety of a nearby alleyway.

The streets suddenly glowed with buzzing pink light as the scout ship performed a heat-seeking scan for its targets. Everyone held their breath as the great ship hovered overhead for what seemed an eternity. Finally, it moved along.

Once the coast was clear, Karai and the Turtles made a break for it. Running side by side with Leo, Karai asked, "What the heck was that thing?"

"I don't know," Leo answered, "but off the top of my head, I'd say they use it for flying and shooting at things."

Then they heard the scout ship circle back. It fired its lasers, barely missing them by an inch.

"It's right on our shells!" Mikey screamed.

Every ninja for herself, Karai thought. Without hesitation, she broke off from the group and darted into the welcoming shadows of an abandoned alley lined with garbage. The pink light searched the street. It was hunting her.

Using her ninja training, Karai stood perfectly still, blending into the night. The ship scanned and scanned but found no trace of her. After another flyby, it finally floated away.

Karai closed her eyes and let out a sigh of relief. She was safe. For now.

A few blocks away, the Turtles had also found sanctuary. They were hiding shell to shell, next to an abandoned car.

Mikey knew making any noise would be a bad idea right now, but he just had to ask Leo something.

"Do you think it knows where we are?" he whispered.

"Yeah, maybe," Leo answered.

Just then, the car they were leaning on was sucked up into the air in a shaft of light. The ship suddenly released it, and the Turtles barrel-rolled out of its path before it landed with a loud crash of broken windshield and twisted metal.

"We gotta get underground!" Donnie yelled.

Leo stepped up, determined to find a way out of this. He saw a manhole cover. An idea was forming.

"I'll draw their fire," he said, unsheathing his shining *katanas.*

Leo rushed out of the shadows, attracting the ship's attention.

He taunted the Kraang by poking fun at their blaster—a glass oval that looked like a giant alien eye. "Over here, Cyclops!"

Using the brick walls to his advantage, Leo bounded into a zigzagging display of somersaults

to dodge the laser blasts.

Seeing their opportunity, the other Turtles popped open the manhole cover. Raph held it in place while Donnie and Mikey climbed down to the safety of the sewers.

"Leo, come on!" Raph shouted.

Leo lobbed a few ninja stars at the scout ship before flinging himself back into the alley. He slid into the chute with Raph, replacing the manhole cover with lightning speed. The ship hovered overhead. It scanned the area, flooding the alley with harsh light.

From behind the sewer grate, the Turtles heard the approaching swarm of police sirens. Maybe they were safe after all.

But right as the cops made it to the scene, the Kraang ship employed an invisibility device and disappeared into thin air.

"Great," Raph groaned. "Because it wasn't scary enough when we could see it."

Police choppers arrived as the minutes passed—one even coming dangerously close to

Karai's hiding place. As a leader of the Foot Clan, she normally hated the sight of the cops.

But not now.

Not after what she had just seen. This situation was bigger than her hatred of the Turtles, bigger than her loyalty to the Shredder and his evil master plan to destroy them. Planet Earth was in danger of an alien threat the likes of which it had never seen. Karai knew she had to do *something* about it.

CHAPTER 3

Later that night, Karai returned home to the Foot Clan's secret lair to tell her father everything. She knew it wouldn't be easy. The Shredder was no normal man. He wasn't used to listening to others' troubles or helping them through tough times. He was a Japanese warlord, the head of the world's oldest ninja clan, and a dark figure feared throughout the underworld.

Had anyone else told him a story about aliens roaming around New York, he would have crushed them with his armored hands simply for wasting his time.

But this was Karai talking. And since she was his only daughter, the Shredder allowed her to speak.

"It's true!" Karai argued, kneeling before her father. "The Kraang are plotting an invasion. I saw the ship myself. They've got some serious hardware."

Shredder was unmoved by this.

"We have to do *something* before it's too late," Karai said, trying to plead with him. And then, in a rare moment of vulnerability, her voice softened. "Father?"

"We shall proceed as planned," Shredder growled.

"But—"

"Tomorrow night, we will receive a shipment of new weapons," he interrupted. "*These* shall help us put an end to the Turtles and Splinter."

"We can deal with

that later," Karai protested. "Didn't you listen to a thing I just—"

Shredder banged his fist down on his throne, yelling, "Karai!"

She flinched.

"You have said your piece. Now you will do as I say," Shredder commanded.

Karai bowed her head. Arguing was clearly getting her nowhere.

"Yes, Father." Karai sighed in frustration.

If her own father wouldn't listen to her, maybe she needed to find someone who would.

CHAPTER 4

Meanwhile, back at the *dojo*, the guys were thinking up a plan of attack. Leo paced the room as Raph threw his *sais* at a tackling dummy for target practice. Each hit was music to his ears.

"That Kraang ship is incredibly dangerous," Leo finally said. "We've got to figure out what it's doing here."

"Or"—Raph coolly spun his *sais,* then took the tackling dummy out with a vicious strike—"we could just skip to the part where we destroy it."

Mikey looked down at the dummy crumpled on the floor. "You're pretty tough when they can't hit back," he teased.

Raph shot his brother a death stare. He didn't

mind a little friendly joshing now and then with his bros, but retreating from the Kraang had really steamed his shell.

The moment Raph raised his fists, Mikey shrank away. He turned his attention back to Leo.

"So what are we waiting for?" Raph asked. "Let's load up the *Shellraiser* and challenge that thing to a rematch."

"First we need a way to find a ship that's invisible," Leo told him.

"I know!" Raph exclaimed. "How about we shoot into the air until we hit it?"

Typical Raph, Leo thought. *Shoot first, ask questions later. . . .*

"That doesn't sound too smart." Leo frowned.

"Yeah, Raph." Mikey giggled. "Not too smart, buddy."

Raph spun around again, ready to pound Mikey—who immediately ducked for cover.

"Actually," Donnie interjected, "Raph's got something there."

"Yeah, Leo," Mikey piped up again, this time

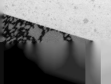

using the tackling dummy like a ventriloquist dummy. "Raph's got something there."

Now it was Leo who stared him down. Mikey was really getting under everyone's shell tonight!

Donnie ignored Mikey's shenanigans and continued his explanation. "Instead of shooting objects, we'll shoot waves of electromagnetic radiation. In other words," he said, holding up an object that looked like a mini satellite dish, ". . . *radar.*"

That got everyone's attention.

"I've built some radar beacons we can set up around town," Donnie went on. "If the ship gets near us, I'll get an alert on my T-Phone."

"Good work, Donnie!" Leo said, relieved to hear some good news for a change. "Come on, guys. Let's split up and place those beacons."

CHAPTER 5

Up on the surface, Leo wasted no time installing his radar beacons throughout the downtown area. He had sent his brothers off to different locations around the city to do the same—and after a night of dealing with Mikey, he welcomed the chance to be on his own for a while.

As he bolted the final radar dish to a rooftop, Leo took out his T-Phone and dialed Donnie.

"Tribeca beacon installed," Leo told him.

"That's the last of them," he heard Donnie say. "Raph and Mikey are finished, too."

Leo smiled. Their work was done for the night. "See you back at the lair," he said. When he hung up his T-Phone, a strange feeling suddenly came over him. It was as if his ninja senses could detect a disturbance in the quiet air. This was no normal breeze. No false alarm. It felt like a person watching his every move. He wasn't imagining it—

He wasn't alone.

Drawing his *katanas* in one swift swoop, Leo spun around just in time to see the metal of his own blade clash with another warrior's sword.

"This is getting old, Karai."

Staring back into his eyes, Karai began to ease up on her blade.

"I want to help you fight the Kraang," she said, trying to explain. As a sign of good faith, she sheathed her sword.

"Really?" Leo asked, still suspicious of her. After some hesitation, he put his *katanas* away and gazed at her.

Could my sworn enemy really have a change of heart? Leo asked himself.

"No, of course not," Leo stated out loud, and then began listing the reasons he shouldn't trust her. "We're enemies. You want to destroy us. You're loyal to the Shredder. Should I keep going?"

"Look, if the Kraang win, we won't have a planet anymore," she said. "That makes our little fight seem pretty pointless, doesn't it?"

"I doubt Shredder would agree," he replied.

Karai couldn't keep her cool anymore. "Shredder is stubborn and shortsighted. He drives me crazy!" she confessed. "What do you say? Work together . . . for now?"

There was a part of Leo that wanted to believe her. But deep down, he knew this could all be a trick.

"Sorry, sister, I can't do it," Leo finally replied. And without saying goodbye, he somersaulted off the rooftop, disappearing into the night.

Karai got the message loud and clear: they were to remain enemies. At least for now.

CHAPTER 6

Leo had never been more confused in his life.

After returning to the lair, he interrupted April's *kunoichi*-training session with Master Splinter to seek his wise counsel. He took a meditative pose, along with his brothers, to ask for his sensei's sage advice.

"I know we shouldn't trust Karai," Leo told them. "But still . . . I got the sense that she really is fed up with Shredder."

"That's probably just what she wants you to think," Raph pointed out.

"I know. . . ." Leo sighed. He stared up at Master Splinter. "Sensei, is there any chance she's for real?"

Splinter stroked his whiskers, deep in thought. As a father, he knew the answer Leo wanted to hear, but as a sensei, he knew it was better to present him with the truth.

"It is possible. Loyalties have been known to shift," Splinter told him. "But the *kunoichi* is trained to use deception to her advantage."

He could see that his students were confused by his wise words, and took pity on them.

"You must trust your instincts," he explained. "But beware the trap of believing something to be true simply because you wish it to be so."

The Turtles stared back at him, speechless.

"So I should trust my instincts . . . unless my instincts are wrong?" Leo asked, trying to make sense of it.

"Exactly," Splinter said.

Pleased with his response, Splinter quietly exited the *dojo,* leaving the Turtles to reflect on his words of wisdom.

"Whoa," Mikey piped up, his mind exhausted from the mental acrobatics of listening to Master

Splinter. "You know it's good advice when you're still confused afterward."

Raph scowled. He didn't have time for Splinter's brain games. His mind was already made up. "Guys—seriously? An alliance with Karai?! No way. Why are we even talking about this?"

"It's too bad we can't trust her," Donnie added. "It would be nice to have a *kunoichi* on our side."

"Um, hello . . . ?" April called out from the back of the *dojo*. "What about me?"

Donnie smiled. "No, I mean a REAL *kunoichi*—"

Realizing he'd just accidentally insulted April in front of everyone, Donnie quickly tried to save face. "I mean, not that you're not a real one," he said, correcting himself. "Just that Karai's better—"

April gasped.

"I mean, um, not *better*," Donnie sputtered, trying to recover. "Just, ah, more experienced."

April shot him a look.

Donnie broke out into a nervous sweat. "Is it hot in here?"

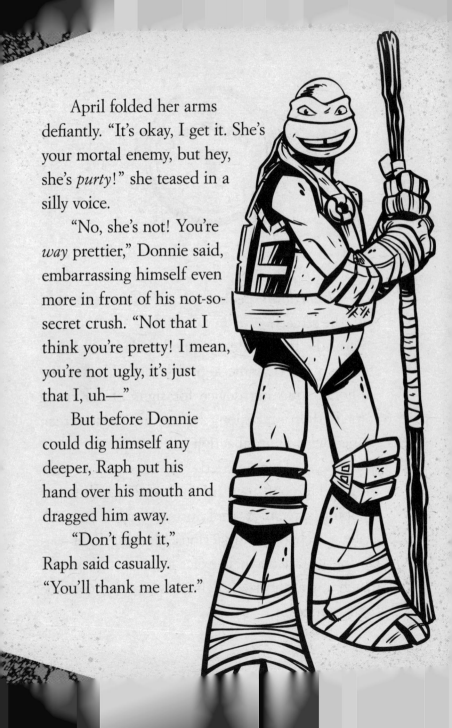

April folded her arms defiantly. "It's okay, I get it. She's your mortal enemy, but hey, she's *purty*!" she teased in a silly voice.

"No, she's not! You're *way* prettier," Donnie said, embarrassing himself even more in front of his not-so-secret crush. "Not that I think you're pretty! I mean, you're not ugly, it's just that I, uh—"

But before Donnie could dig himself any deeper, Raph put his hand over his mouth and dragged him away.

"Don't fight it," Raph said casually. "You'll thank me later."

CHAPTER

7

The *Shellraiser* peeled out of the sewers and onto the streets.

Inside, the Turtles manned their usual battle stations while Donnie kept his eyes glued to the T-Phone's tracking device for signs of a Kraang ship. It didn't take long before his radar screen flashed with unusual activity.

"Guys!" Donnie cried. "I think I've got something!" He confirmed his findings on a different mapping screen. A knot formed in his stomach as he watched—a mysterious blinking light was closing in fast on their exact location. "It doesn't match any authorized flight patterns! It's gotta be the Kraang ship!"

"Or . . . Santa!" Mikey declared hopefully.

Suddenly a flying, squid-shaped alien spacecraft materialized in front of them. Its pulse cannon glowed, aiming right at them.

"Aww, it's the Kraang ship," Mikey groaned. "That's a bummer."

The Kraang ship nose-dived and unleashed a barrage of energy blasts.

"Move it, Leo!" Raph barked.

Leo punched the gas. "Hang on to your shells!" he shouted, swerving the *Shellraiser* around an explosive burst. With another pulse-pounding boom, the interior of the van rattled violently around them.

Driving at top speed, Leo ignored the Kraang's lasers and stayed as focused as he could on the road ahead. Donnie checked out the *Shellraiser*'s surveillance cam—the video feed showed the Kraang ship gaining ground. The pulse cannon fired another shot.

"Mikey, we need an escape route!" Leo said.

Mikey swung the magnifying glass down at

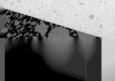

his navigation station. He quickly scanned the map for a way out. "Take the alley on the right!" he suggested.

Leo spun the wheel and skidded into the alley—which was blocked by a ten-foot-tall concrete wall.

Leo slumped in the driver's seat. "It's a dead end."

Mikey checked his map again. Then he blushed when he realized his mistake. "I mean, *don't* take the alley on the right!"

But it was too late. Leo looked at his rearview mirror and saw only one thing— the scout ship! It was hovering right behind them, blocking their only exit.

They were cornered by the Kraang!

CHAPTER 8

The Kraang ship opened fire. A pink electric bolt of energy pierced through the *Shellraiser* as easily as a knife cutting into butter.

Everything inside the van shook. Sparks bounced off the walls, stinging and shocking the Turtles as they tried to figure out a way to escape.

"Any ideas, guys?" Leo yelled over the deafening sound of the Kraang laser.

"Just one," Raph replied, angrily gnashing his teeth. He stalked over to Mikey's station and punched him repeatedly for getting them into this mess.

More pieces of the van began to smolder under the terrible beam from the laser.

As the *Shellraiser* sizzled, another strange

vehicle sliced through the sky, hopping rooftop to rooftop. It was a sleek custom motorbike: the Dragon Chopper!

And Karai was in the driver's seat.

She drove her bike off the edge of the building, then leaped from it, somersaulting through the air.

The bike crashed to the sidewalk as Karai unsheathed her ninja blade. She landed on the ship and stabbed it in one graceful, fluid move.

The Kraang ship started to malfunction. Inside the cockpit, the alien pilots exclaimed in garbled Kraang speak, "This is that which is known as not good."

The ship stopped firing on the Turtles and suddenly shot upward, weaving this way and that through the sky.

Inside the van, the Turtles were shocked by what they'd just seen.

"That was Karai!" Leo said, reversing the *Shellraiser.* "We've got to go back and help her!"

He floored the van, now in hot pursuit of the Kraang ship.

And Karai.

Raph ran over to Leo, trying to talk some sense into him. "She can take care of herself. Let's put some distance between that thing and us!"

"No!" Leo shouted. He was determined, keeping his eyes on the ship and ignoring the flashing warning lights on the *Shellraiser*'s control console.

"But the *Shellraiser* can't take another attack right now!" Donnie cried from the main control panel.

"Then I'll do it myself!" Leo announced furiously. He unbuckled his seat belt and switched places with Raph. "Drive!" he ordered.

Leo climbed to the back of the van. "I'll meet you back underground," he instructed, opening a secret hatch. Inside was a sleek, one-person motorcycle known as the Stealth Bike.

"Hey, the Stealth Bike's *my* thing," Raph moaned.

Leo was not in the mood. He mounted the Stealth Bike and glowered at Raph. "Well, now your thing is sucking it up," he said.

"Hey . . . that's *my* thing!" Donnie protested.

Leo shut the hatch and left them behind.

The *Shellraiser*'s front fender opened up, and Leo rolled out on the Stealth Bike.

He was a Turtle on a mission.

CHAPTER 9

Karai was three hundred feet in the air, holding on to the Kraang ship for dear life. Her ninja sword, still buried deep in the ship, was the only thing keeping her from falling to her doom.

She knew she had to bring the ship down if she wanted to survive. But how? She didn't know the first thing about fighting aliens, and with only one hand free for action, she was battling at half strength. She punched the exposed wiring of the ship, hoping for something—*anything*—to stop it.

"THIS . . . is . . . so . . . NOT . . . fun!" she yelled between punches.

One of her power punches shorted something out. With a boom, the ship spun erratically,

careening off buildings. Karai struggled to keep hold of the blade. She knew if she fell from this height, it wouldn't be pretty.

She wasn't aware that something was following her. Something fast enough to keep pace with the Kraang ship. Something with a roaring engine.

Karai could feel her hands slipping. Then her wrist gave out. She slid off.

Falling.

Screaming.

Gasping at the sudden sight of the Stealth Bike racing down the city street!

Leo sped up the front of a parked car, launching the Stealth Bike into the air just in time to catch Karai safely in his arms.

Before she knew what was happening, the bike landed securely on the road. Leo stared into her eyes. "Are you okay?" he asked, the wind whipping past them.

"Yeah," she answered, catching her breath. "Are you?"

"I'm fine."

As he sped away from the ship, Leo could feel Karai trembling. In that moment, she didn't seem like his enemy. She seemed like a friend, a scared friend who needed help.

"I'm not really good about saying thank you," she said softly.

The moment was cut short by a pulse blast from the Kraang ship!

Another energy blast rained down, exploding pieces of the road into burning chunks. Leo activated the Stealth Bike's hidden shell-shield, which made them nearly invisible to the Kraang's scanners.

"And . . . ?" Leo said expectantly.

"That was it," she told him.

Well, Leo thought, *maybe she didn't change that much after all.*

Up ahead, through a cloud of flying debris, Leo saw the perfect hiding spot. He drifted into a pocket of shadows on a side street, enhancing the bike's invisibility even more.

The Kraang ship did a flyby, scanning for them. It closed in on their area of the street. Leo and Karai held their breath, doing their best to remain hidden behind the shell-shield and to remain calm.

After the scanner failed to find any life-forms, one Kraang pilot decided to call it quits. "Kraang will find them at a time which is sooner than a time that is later and that time . . . is later."

Leo and Karai sat in tense silence, watching as the ship flew away.

They each took a breath, relieved.

They exchanged smiles.

CHAPTER 10

A short while later, Leo whisked Karai away to the safest place in the city: underground. They drove through the pitch-black subway tunnels until the Stealth Bike's headlights illuminated what looked like an abandoned subway car in the distance.

It was the *Shellraiser*.

Leo hit the brakes and docked the bike inside.

The van's hydraulic hatch opened with a loud clanging sound. To the other Turtles' surprise, Leo wasn't the only one boarding the *Shellraiser*. Karai was right behind him.

"We're back!" Leo announced.

A look of complete shock washed over Raph's

face. "You brought her inside?! Dude, she'll see all our gear!"

Looking around the inside of the *Shellraiser*, Karai didn't even want to dignify that with a response. All she could see was recycled garbage and a glow-in-the-dark dessert cone. "Yeah, 'cause if Shredder finds out you have an ice cream lamp, it is over," she mocked.

The other Turtles were unsure how to react. They all looked to Leo.

"Karai just risked her life to save us," Leo argued. "She's earned a little trust. Let's hear her out."

"You're the boss," Raph grumbled, but he clearly wasn't happy about it.

Karai knew they had every reason not to trust her. An apology wouldn't be enough. She needed to prove she was trustworthy.

"You guys need my help. You really think you can shoot down an alien warship with

garbage?" she said, pointing out the van's trash-shooting cannon.

Donnie piped up to defend his creation. "*Compressed* garbage!" he corrected her.

"And manhole covers!" Mikey added.

"My point is, to take out a ship like that, you need a *real* weapon," Karai told them.

Raph sneered. "Oh, yeah? Like what?"

"What if I got you a shoulder-fired missile launcher?" Karai asked.

Real military firepower? That got Raph's attention. "I'm starting to like her," he joked.

Donnie couldn't believe what he was hearing. Unlike Raph, the promise of stuff blowing up wasn't enough to sway him to Karai's side. "Where are you going to get a shoulder-fired missile launcher?" he asked.

"Shredder, of course," she replied.

Karai's answer met an uncomfortable silence as the guys silently shivered at the mention of their archenemy's name. The Shredder didn't exactly seem like the giving type.

Mikey spoke up first. "Uh, we are talking about the same Shredder, right? Big dude . . . lots of blades . . . really hates us?"

"Yeah," Raph agreed. "Something tells me he's not going to share his toys with us."

"He won't know about it," Karai said. "He's buying a big shipment of weapons down at the docks tomorrow night. All we need to do is sneak in and help ourselves."

Raph smirked. "Anyone else smell a trap?"

Mikey raised his hand sheepishly. "Sorry, that was me," he said, quickly waving away the air around his station.

"Why would I trap you?" Karai asked. "You're the only ones who know what the Kraang are really up to."

"True," Donnie responded. "But . . . you don't really have the best track record."

Karai glanced around the *Shellraiser*. The Turtles still weren't convinced.

"Fine," Karai said, knowing there only one thing left to do to prove she was more than her villainous past. "I'll get you the missile launcher myself," she declared resolutely.

Leo's jaw nearly hit the floor. "You're really willing to steal from Shredder?"

"Look, these things have to be stopped. If Shredder's not going to do anything about it, then I will," she said defiantly.

Leo locked eyes with her. She was serious. He looked to the other Turtles, each nodding approval of this new plan.

"All right, here's the deal," Leo said. "You get us the missile launcher and we'll team up."

Leo and Karai shook on it.

An unlikely truce had begun.

CHAPTER 11

After returning home to the lair, the Turtles each found different ways to unwind. Donnie read magazines on the couch. Leo practiced his *kata* on the tackling dummy. Mikey and Raph played *Space Heroes* pinball.

"I can't believe we're getting a missile launcher!" Mikey exclaimed. "What should we blow up first?"

"Uh, the Kraang ship?" Raph flatly replied.

"Oh, right! What should we blow up *second*?"

Wham! Leo kicked the tackling dummy with all his might. Despite the relaxing vibe in the *dojo,* he seemed to be getting more and more anxious with every practice hit.

"That's *if* Karai can pull it off," Leo said,

hitting the dummy again with a one-two strike.

Donnie watched Leo with dawning recognition. "Are you worried about your *girlfriend*?" he teased. He chuckled to himself, thankful to be the one dishing it out for a change, and then added, "I see why you guys do that now. It's kinda fun."

Leo ignored that. His mind was focused on retrieving the missile launcher from the docks and the risks surrounding it.

"It isn't gonna be easy," he said. "Shredder will be there, too."

"Hey . . . you're right," Raph said, putting the pieces together. "For once, we know where Shredder's going to be ahead of time! Which means . . . we could set a trap *for him*!"

"What?" Leo stared at him in disbelief. "We made a deal with Karai. We can't just go behind her back. This is about that Kraang ship. They want to take us out!"

"So does Shredder!" Raph replied quickly. "This may be our only chance to take him by surprise. Are we really going to pass that up?"

As much as Leo hated to admit it, he knew Raph was right. He hated the idea of breaking his promise to Karai and dishonoring the ninja code of truth. But he knew that this truce was only temporary and that his family was forever.

All eyes were on him.

Leo nodded. "Let's take down Shredder."

CHAPTER 12

The shipyard docks at night were one of the few places in New York City that didn't hustle and bustle. A wall of steel crates, stacked on top of one another nearly twenty feet high, made the pier look like an indestructible fortress. At this late hour, the docks were empty, and the only sound was the river lapping back and forth.

So Karai was careful to move in silence.

Up ahead, she spied the figure of a tall man, dressed in a Russian military uniform. He appeared to be alone, standing quietly next to an unmarked car. He looked normal, except for one peculiar feature—he had a diamond eye.

Karai stomped as loudly as she could to

distract the ominous soldier.

Thud!

The man with the diamond eye turned to look at her, as Shredder and members of the Foot Clan snuck up behind him.

"Where is the shipment?" Shredder growled.

At Shredder's signal, a Foot Soldier came forward with a briefcase. The man with the diamond eye opened it. He smiled when he saw the golden glow coming from inside.

"I'll inspect the merchandise," Karai said.

The man with the

diamond eye looked at Shredder. "Don't you trust me?" he asked in a thick Russian accent. "We are old friends."

"Then you won't mind keeping me company while she checks," Shredder replied.

The man with the diamond eye got comfortable. It was clear he wasn't going anywhere for a little while.

While Karai took a closer look at the weapons, the Turtles were gathered on another stack of crates nearby, spying on Shredder and his crew. They were waiting for the perfect opportunity to strike with a perfect weapon: a modified water-balloon launcher.

And who was better at launching random objects than Mikey?

"Aim for his armor," Donnie recommended, holding up a round explosive device. "This electro-grenade will use the metal as a conductor to amplify the shock."

Donnie never got a response. Instead, Mikey just stared off into space. "How much of that did I need to understand?" he finally asked.

"Just aim for his armor," Donnie translated.

Mikey smiled. "Got it!"

"You sure we should trust Mikey with this?" Raph asked, bracing for the worst.

"When it comes to water-balloon launchers, he's the best in the business," Leo replied, holding one end of the launcher.

Mikey loaded the electro-grenade in place and pulled back to aim. As he set his sights on Shredder, Leo and Raph kept watch on the meeting below.

They saw Karai snooping around the missile launcher crate as planned. And just as she was about to swipe one, she looked up and saw the Turtles. It took her a few moments to register what was about to happen, but when she did, the surprise on her face was evident. She was being double-crossed.

"*Booyakasha,* Shred-head!" Mikey whispered, releasing his grip and launching the electro-grenade.

Karai raced toward Shredder.

"Look out!" she screamed, tackling Shredder out of the way.

The electro-grenade missed them and—*ka-blam!*—it blasted the man with the diamond eye instead.

Raph couldn't believe what she had just done. "Are you kidding me?" he griped.

Mikey paused, taking a long look at Karai. "I do not understand that woman."

A moment later, Karai rose to her feet, furious. *How could they do this to me?* she thought. She picked up the missile launcher—the very weapon she had planned to steal *for them*—and aimed at the Turtles. Without hesitation, she squeezed the trigger and a deafening roar came from the weapon.

"Incoming!" Leo yelled.

BLAM!

The Turtles

were blown into the air before they plummeted through a cloud of black smoke to the docks below. Pain shot through their bodies.

Raph was the first to shake it off. He took a look at the flames above them, trying to assess the damage. "Well, this can't get much worse," he said.

He turned, hearing a little *beep-beep-beep* behind him. It was Donnie's T-Phone.

Donnie finally sat up, half conscious, and checked his phone. His eyes widened in terror. "The radar! The Kraang ship is nearby."

They looked up into the night sky. It seemed to twist into an unnatural blur. The outline of a mysterious shape began to form. Then, in a flash of light, the Kraang warship appeared.

CHAPTER 13

Leo rose from the rubble and saw the ship looming over them. "Fall back, guys!" he commanded.

"No argument here!" Donnie agreed.

The Turtles broke into a run, unaware that someone was storming after them. They dashed through the shipyard, trying to find a way out. But the tall stacks of shipping crates turned the docks into a maze with walls of steel at every turn. No one wanted to say it, but the more they ran, the more lost they became.

Leo spotted light nearby and, taking a chance, turned toward it. It was a dead end! They were boxed in by steel crates, with no escape.

There was a clanging noise behind them. It

seemed to be moving and was growing louder and louder by the second. Then everything went eerily quiet.

They turned to see who was blocking their path—and found themselves face to face with a hulking man with a suit made of razor-sharp spikes.

Shredder!

"Tell me where Splinter is, and I'll let you live long enough to watch him perish," he snarled.

Before he could say another word, there was a rumbling from overhead. A massive flying object crested the wall of crates, casting a shadow over them all. It was the Kraang ship. It circled above them, its tentacles probing around the area and scanning for life-forms.

"That thing again?" Leo said. "Great timing."

The Shredder couldn't believe what he was seeing. He just stared at it, almost hypnotized.

The Kraang ship unloaded a barrage of zig-zagging energy streams at them. Debris flew up in the clouds of dust and cement as each electric pink bolt ricocheted off the steel crates and burned the concrete under their feet. The Turtles managed to flip out of the way to safety.

The ship unleashed another energy stream—this one slicing toward Shredder. The cunning ninja warlord threw open the doors of a nearby shipping crate and disappeared inside its protective steel. The stream flew right past him.

Through the chaos, Leo finally saw their opportunity to escape: their exit path was now clear. And better still—Shredder had stuffed himself inside a giant crate. Their ultimate enemy had unknowingly laid his very own trap!

All Leo had to do was wait for his moment.

He saw the ship suddenly ascend, swooping around in the distance to begin another attack. That was when he rushed into action, darting out into the line of fire to slam the lock shut on Shredder's crate.

"Come on!" Leo urged the other Turtles as he ran to safety.

Donnie and the others started after him—right as Shredder's blades ripped through the solid

steel wall of his crate. With the *screeeeeech* of steel on steel, Shredder slashed his way out, carving a hole big enough for him to climb through.

Once he stepped out into the light, it became clear to the Shredder that the Turtles were completely walled in—steel crates stacked twenty feet high surrounded them on three sides, and he was blocking their only exit path.

"We'll catch up to you later!" Donnie cried out to Leo.

And Donnie, Raph, and Mikey cowered as Shredder stood before them.

Unaware that his brothers were trapped, Leo scrambled through the labyrinth of shipping crates until he found a clearing. Suddenly, an acrobatic figure somersaulted into his path. It was Karai.

"I thought you were better than this! I thought you were my friend! How could you betray me? You're just as shortsighted and obsessed as Shredder!" she screamed angrily.

Leo tried to reason with her. "You said your-self how bad Shredder is! Why are you protecting him? You said he's driving you crazy!"

"He drives me crazy . . . because he's my father."

"Your *father*? Shredder is your father? You're Shredder's *daughter*?!"

Leo couldn't believe what he was hearing. All this time, he'd thought she was just a talented ninja who fell in with the wrong crowd. But it made sense now. He always chose family first . . . and so did she. They would never be able to join forces.

A second later, something else came between them—*literally!* The Kraang ship soared past, fir-ing on anything in its sights.

Leo looked back to Karai. "We've gotta stop that thing!"

"Our deal's off!" she cried. "You want a feud? You've got one!"

CHAPTER 14

Donnie, Raph, and Mikey tried to hold their own against Shredder. He seemed to know all of their *kata* combos, dispatching them without even breaking a sweat. Even with three-on-one attacks, the devious leader of the Foot Clan was showing no signs of slowing down.

They flung throwing stars at him, but Shredder was simply too fast for their attack. He dodged the sharp spinners expertly, the little projectiles whistling past him and clanking off the crates behind him.

Frustrated, the Turtles charged forward again.

Raph stepped up, swinging his *sais* in anger. He was tired of running from the Shredder. He landed a few strikes—and then old Shred-head surprised him with a power punch to the stomach. Raph was wrecked!

Now it was Mikey's turn. He flung the rest of this throwing stars and then executed a series of *nunchuck* speed attacks. Shredder quickly countered them all and then booted him backward.

Donnie thought out his next move carefully. Clearly, a head-on assault wasn't going to work—so he went airborne! He jumped from crate to crate, using the steel stacks to propel him into a power arc. He sprang at Shredder. His *bo* staff ready for smacking. But the martial arts master sent him flying with a single blow.

Knowing that he had the Turtles on the run, Shredder menacingly moved forward. His arm blades extended, ready to slice and dice. As he got closer, his voice seemed to boom from behind his mask.

"Prepare to learn why they call me the Shredder," the masked villain hissed as he moved forward, his cold shadow falling across the Turtles.

Donnie, Raph, and Mikey weren't the only ones staring down a blade. Elsewhere on the docks, Karai's ninja sword was slicing just inches away from Leo's face.

Karai wasn't playing around this time. Leo could tell she was really trying to wound him. He wondered if his bros had gotten free, but he really had no way of knowing. All he could do was press on, parrying Karai's attacks as best he could.

She got him with a stunner: a knee to the chin. The world went blurry for Leo, and when his vision finally normalized, he saw her disarm him, knocking one of his *katanas* away. She had him up against the wall. Then the familiar hum of the Kraang ship caught her attention.

It swooped in, blaster blazing! Karai backflipped out of the line of fire, ducking behind another crate for cover.

When the blaster smoke lifted, she peeked her head out to check if the coast was clear.

The ship was gone—and so was Leo.

She watched as his silhouette disappeared among the crates. And she felt the anger rising up in the back of her throat.

He had survived her sword . . . this time.

Donnie, Raph, and Mikey picked themselves up, preparing to battle Shredder again. They were tired and hurt, but ready for another chance to put a dent in the evil one's armor.

Suddenly, the Kraang ship screamed low, nearly taking them all out. In its wake, the Turtles were whipped back to the ground, as was Shredder. When they looked up, they saw the ship bank, heading back for more target practice.

During their close encounter, no one had noticed a figure standing atop the crates, pointing something large at the sky.

It was Leo! And he was holding one of the missile launchers he had freshly swiped from one of the weapon crates. He looked through the

The Turtles are on patrol, looking for evil Kraang activity.

Karai drops in for a visit.

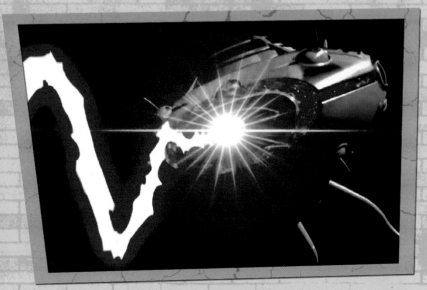

A Kraang ship attacks!

Karai wants to team up with the Turtles to defeat the Kraang. Can she be trusted, or is she helping Shredder?

The Kraang strike the *Shellraiser.*

Karai to the rescue!

Karai tells the Turtles about a weapons shipment
Shredder is getting that could destroy the Kraang ship.

A man with a diamond eye brings Shredder
his weapons.

The Turtles try to foil
Shredder's plan.

Leo and Karai are
enemies again!

A captured Kraang-droid reveals that
April O'Neil has secret powers.

April trains to be a *kunoichi* with Splinter.

The Turtles search for the underwater Kraang base in their submarine.

"Seriously, Donnie, a submarine powered by bicycles?" Leo asks.

April makes a new friend at lunch.

The Turtles sneak into the underwater base.

April learns that her new friend is Karai.

A sea monster traps the Turtles, and Mikey
takes it for a ride.

April tests her ninja skills on Karai.

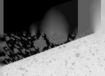

weapon's scope, putting the Kraang ship right in its crosshairs. Squeezing the trigger as hard as he could, Leo fired the missile that was about to put an end to this whole mess.

Ka-blam! The rocket flew out, arcing upward toward the ship. Inside the cockpit, radar screens screamed with warning signals. The missile was fast approaching.

Inside, one of the Kraang brain-things had enough time to say: "This is definitely that which is known as not good—"

As the rocket exploded, it blew a massive hole in the side of the ship. The craft plummeted toward the docks on a crash course, smoke spiraling out behind it. On its way down, it narrowly missed mowing everyone over—

Except for Shredder. The runaway ship hit him head-on, then pulled him under its hull and rolled him over the edge of the docks into the depths of the river.

"Father!" Karai yelled. She sheathed her sword and dove into the icy waves to save him.

Leo wanted to wait there as long as it took, watching to see if Karai surfaced safely. But his brothers were urging him to leave the shipyard while they still had the chance. Their work was done here. They had saved the city from the Kraang and gotten the better of Shredder.

But at what cost? Leo thought. Yes, the battle was over . . . but so was any hope of a friendship with Karai.

After a few more moments, he left the docks, hearing nothing but the waves lapping behind him.

CHAPTER 15

Later, miles away from the docks, the Turtles found a secluded rooftop where they could regroup and catch their breath. Leo broke away from the pack and stepped up to the edge, looking out over the city. Before him were people out and about, enjoying their lives, going to dinner, laughing on the street. They were all safe now because of him.

But for a hero who had just KO'd the Kraang on behalf of New York, he felt pretty glum.

Donnie made his way past the other Turtles and tried to comfort him. "Leo, it's not *that* bad. You blew up the Kraang ship!"

"But I also blew our chance to get Karai on our side," Leo replied solemnly.

"Look, she's Shredder's daughter!" Raph reminded him. "She's his blood! She was never going to be on our side."

Leo just stared into space pensively. "Maybe you're right." And then, with Master Splinter's teachings echoing in his head, he realized, "Maybe I was just believing what I wanted to."

Mikey cautiously approached the group. He wasn't one for serious talks, but he wanted to comfort his big bro any way he could, which meant he had to dig deep for his most stirring and emotional memory. "I've been there, dude," he said. "For me, it was leprechauns."

Leo turned to Mikey. "Are you seriously comparing what I'm going through to the time you found out leprechauns aren't real?!"

Mikey looked stunned.

Leo noticed Donnie and Raph in the background, frantically waving their hands around.

But it was too late. "Leprechauns aren't real?" Mikey moaned.

Leo groaned. This was going to be a long night.

Meanwhile, back at the docks, Karai finally emerged from the icy waters, gasping for air. She could barely move her arms and legs, but using the little strength she had left, she hauled Shredder safely ashore.

"Well done, Karai," he said, breathing hard. Shredder had never been prouder of his daughter, or more grateful for her actions. So he decided to reward her bravery with a gift.

"I found something for you," he coughed, pulling out a squirming Kraang brain-thing he'd pulled from the depths of the sunken warship. He held it upside down by its slimy tentacles.

It squealed.

Karai took one look and recoiled in horror. She had never seen anything so hideous.

But the Shredder saw things a little differently.

He smiled wickedly behind his metal mask, forming a new evil plan. He turned to Karai and said, "You always wanted a pet."

CHAPTER 16

The Shredder wanted answers. But the disembodied Kraang could only make high-pitched shrieking noises.

"Why were you hunting the Turtles?" Shredder demanded.

But all he got in return was a *hisssss*!

If the slimy little alien knew how to speak English, it never let on. All it did was writhe in Shredder's grip and try to squirm away.

Karai stood by her father's side, amused. "They don't talk much outside their little houses," she explained, tapping on the junked parts of a nearby damaged Kraang-droid exoskeleton.

Shredder studied the mess of robotics before

him. The droid had clearly suffered a nasty spill—severed metal limbs, exposed wiring, a decaying face, and an empty slot where a "stomach" would normally be.

Shredder decided to start there. He jammed the alien blob inside the exoskeleton. Lights began to glow all over the droid's body. With beeps and whirs, the system rebooted and the brainlike Kraang calmed itself and closed its eyes contentedly.

Then, through a malfunctioning voice chip, it finally spoke.

"Kraang is lacking the knowledge to answer the questions that the one known as Shredder is asking of Kraang."

Shredder looked over at Karai, dumbfounded. "Do they all speak like this?" he asked her.

"Even if Kraang is possessing the knowledge," the droid continued, "the one known as Shredder will never be getting that knowledge from Kraang."

Karai could tell the little Kraang was annoying her father. And she thought it was funny. "You didn't have any other plans for today, did you?" She smirked.

"Let's try this again," Shredder growled. Then, in a frightening show of force, he shot out his arm blade—and held it up to the Kraang's eyeball.

"Why were you hunting the Turtles?" Shredder snarled.

The little brain blob cowered in terror as it spoke through the droid: "The ones known as the Turtles are protecting the life-form needed by Kraang, the one known as April O'Neil."

Shredder paused. *Who?*

"Who is this April O'Neil?" he barked.

"She is the one known as the one. She is the link which is missing in the plan, which is the plan of Kraang."

"So this April O'Neil is at the center of everything," Karai said.

"Then perhaps we can use her to draw the Turtles out of hiding," Shredder replied. And with that, a new evil plan was set in motion. "Karai, find this girl and bring her to me."

17

While Shredder was talking to the Kraang, deep underground in the sewers, the Turtles were trash-talking each other!

It was a ninja sparring exercise with everyone partnering up: Master Splinter with April, his *kunoichi*-in-training; Leo with Donnie; and finally, Raph with Mikey.

Though it certainly wasn't traditional *ninjutsu,* talking smack was allowed—a fact that was not lost on Raph, who was trying to taunt Mikey into making the first move. "Whatcha gonna do? Whatcha gonna do?" he scoffed, readying his *sais* for a surprise attack.

Mikey stepped back, hesitating—and Raph

leaped through the air for his trademark nose-dive tackle. It looked to be a direct hit . . .

. . . until Mikey seized an opportunity at the last second. Falling backward, he caught Raph with his feet and flipped him over.

It was a *ninjutsu* stroke of genius. And Mikey knew it!

"*Booyakasha*! You got faced!" he told Raph. And then he held up his hands, pretending to play an instrument. "Thought you had me, but I played you like a trombone. *Waah-waaaaaah!*"

Raph didn't take Mikey's celebrating lightly. His face twisted into an angry knot before he lunged at Mikey and wrapped him in a bear hug.

"Playtime's over, tough guy!" Raph said, squeezing harder.

"Put me down!" Mikey pleaded. "Uncle!"

"I don't see you tapping out," Raph said.

"Can't . . . move . . . my . . . arms," Mikey wheezed.

"Then tap your horrible middle toe."

Against his will, Mikey wiggled his toe, and Raph put him down.

Mikey looked down at his middle toe apologetically. "Don't worry, Stubby," he whispered. "You're not as horrible as he says."

"Michelangelo!" Master Splinter called from the back of the *dojo*. "Why did you give up so easily?"

"There was nothing I could do," he replied.

"There is *always* something you can do. Observe."

Splinter approached Raphael, saying *"Kannuki jime,"* Japanese for "Attack me from behind."

A nervous look crossed Raph's face. Whenever their wise sensei began a demonstration with that phrase, it usually meant pain was soon to follow. April and the other Turtles gathered around to watch.

With a gulp, Raph wrapped his arms around Master Splinter and lifted him off the floor.

"The key is to unbalance your opponent," Master Splinter instructed.

"But how?" Mikey asked.

"However you can. For example—"

At that exact moment, their sensei did the unthinkable: he licked Raph on the head! Instantly grossed out, Raph dropped him—which Master Splinter used as an opportunity to smack Raph to the floor with a swift flick of his rat tail.

"You see?" he asked the group. "There is always a way." He took a brief pause, then spat, clearly disgusted by the aftertaste on his tongue.

"And you need to take a bath," he added, pointing at Raphael.

CHAPTER 18

Raph had been hoping to kick his night off with an intense video-game marathon. But Leo got to the television first, which meant they were all forced to sit back and endure another episode of his favorite TV show, *Space Heroes*.

So Raph and Mikey munched mindlessly on a pizza as Leo sat up front, entranced by the action-packed scene on screen: A landing party of inter-galactic explorers was under attack by a Martian beast, but Captain Ryan, the show's main charac-ter, refused to step in and save them. He believed his crew would never learn to take care of them-selves if they always relied on him to rescue them after every mission.

Leo could definitely relate to that.

Just as the episode was about to launch into its final scene, the Turtles heard a voice from the back of the lair.

"Hey, guys!" It was Donnie, peeking out from the shadows of his secret lab. "Guess what April and I have been up to?" he said with a shy smile.

Leo, Raph, and Mikey stared back in silence.

"Analyzing sewage!" Donnie announced.

"Who says you don't know how to show a girl a good time?" Raph smugly replied.

Donnie ignored Raphael and led them all back to his subterranean laboratory, where April waited under the overhead lights with a beaker of bluish liquid.

"April and I were going through some files on the Kraang storage device," Donnie explained, nodding toward the alien object they'd recovered a few weeks ago from T.C.R.I. "We found out they're using a special process to change Earth's water into . . . Kraang water."

"They've already started the process," April

added. "We found a low concentration of Kraang chemicals in the sewage."

Raph was trying to follow, but it was all techno-babble to him. "I take it that's a bad thing?" he asked.

Donnie decided it was time to demonstrate. He pulled out a piece of pizza he'd pilfered from the living room and held it over the cloudy liquid. "Watch what happens when I dip this slice of Mikey's shrimp and sardine pizza into pure Kraang water."

Mikey watched in horror as the alien fluid destroyed his slice of pizza, dissolving it into greenish goo. He screamed at Donnie, *"How do you sleep at night?!"*

Donnie ignored Mikey. "Presently, there's only a tiny bit in the water supply, but the concentration is increasing. Which means—"

"Every slice of pizza in New York will be destroyed?!" Mikey exclaimed.

"Along with anyone who uses water." April told him.

"I don't want to live in a world without pizza!"

Mikey cried, slamming his hands down on the table, which accidentally knocked the test beaker over! The acidic blue liquid inside splashed up into the air like a geyser.

"April, look out!" Donnie cried.

April tried to move out of the way. But the Kraang water sloshed onto her arm.

The Turtles sprang to her aid, expecting the worst. A million thoughts were running through their heads at once: Would she mutate? Would her arm melt off?

April winced, bracing for a horrible burning sensation unlike any in the known universe—

But the pain never came. She opened her eyes. The mysterious Kraang water simply rolled off her forearm, leaving only a harmless, bright blue stain on her sleeve. Nothing hurt. She was fine. April and the Turtles all breathed a sigh of relief.

Except Donnie.

He was grateful, of course, but seriously per-plexed. Judging by the tests, that liquid should have eaten right through her skin. But April didn't

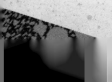

have a scratch on her—as if she was somehow immune.

"Nothing happened to you?" Donnie asked in amazement.

Mikey tried to offer a reasonable explanation. "Maybe it's because she's not made of pizza."

A *beep-beep-beep* startled the group back into the moment. On one of Donnie's Kraang trackers, a homing beacon was flashing on a digital map screen.

"Look! It's the scanners located at the Kraang facility transforming the water supply! Which is right here!" Donnie exclaimed, pointing out a highlighted area on-screen. "We gotta stop it!"

"Looks like we've got a mission," Leo announced. "You coming, April?"

"Sounds like a blast, but unfortunately . . .," April began, noticing the beacon's unusual location on the map, ". . . it's on the bottom of the East River. And equally unfortunate, I have an essay due."

She grabbed her book bag. "Plus, I wouldn't

mind a little human food," she added.

"Pizza's human food!" Mikey argued.

"Not the way you eat it," she responded, starting to make her way out of the lab.

"Whoa, you're going topside?" Donnie asked with a hint of concern. "You're bringing your T-Phone, right?"

"Donnie, don't worry. I'll be fine," April said, trying her best to appear confident to the guys. But deep down inside, she felt shaken up, almost . . . *unnatural*. She looked down at the alien stain on her sleeve, realizing she had a lot to think about. Alone.

"So, Donnie," Leo said as Donnie watched her leave the lab. "How are we gonna get out there?"

A mischievous smile crossed Donnie's face. "Don't worry, guys. I've been working on something that is pretty awesome."

Soon after, the Turtles found themselves on wheels—just not the kind they were expecting.

"This . . . is not . . . awesome!" Raph moaned.

He and his brothers were all working up a sweat, pedaling exercise bikes to help propel Donnie's latest and greatest creation: the Turtle Sub! The submarine, designed to look like a giant sea turtle on the outside, creaked under the pressure of the East River as they piloted it thirty feet below the surface.

"Seriously, Donnie?" Leo said, huffing as he pedaled. "A submarine powered by bicycles?"

"You know what would have been more efficient?" Raph asked, straining. "Swimming!"

"Hey, pipe down, guys!" Donnie was clearly insulted. "Kinetic energy is the only way to charge the engines," he explained. And then, reaching up to a console of switches, he added, "Which should be done right about now!"

With the push of a button, the Turtle Sub's engines suddenly hummed to life. The Turtles, spent and exhausted from their marathon of pedaling, sat back to recover and catch their breath.

Except Donnie. He was at the helm, steering the armored Sub through the murky depths toward a Kraang signal he'd been tracking.

After a few moments, Leo gathered whatever leftover strength he had and dismounted from the bike. "We're almost there," he said gratefully. He collected himself and took the role of captain. "Up, periscope!" he commanded.

A ramshackle periscope, constructed from camera parts and an old toilet seat, swung down from the rafters. Leo winced at the stains caked on it. He did not want to put his face on that.

Unfortunately, it was the only periscope on board.

With a scowl, he leaned in, careful not to touch the toilet parts. He looked through the viewer at the underwater scenery ahead.

The East River was a mysterious mix of moving light and shadows.

Well, one *very big* shadow—a misshapen form that disappeared and reappeared, circling the Sub. It moved quickly, scissoring the water with what looked like a pronged tail.

"Uh, Donnie?" Leo called from the periscope. "Any chance this Kraang facility looks like a giant sea mutant?"

Donnie looked through a porthole and saw the creature for himself. "Oh, that's not a mutant," he said flatly. "Based on his physiology, I'd say the Kraang brought him here from Dimension X."

Leo shuddered. *Another alien?*

"How is that less horrifying?" he asked.

"It's not," Donnie replied nonchalantly. "I just like to be accurate."

Raph stepped up to the periscope to see this beast for himself. It looked like an underwater dinosaur, with its long serpentlike tail, massive stomach, elongated neck, and tiny head that flashed rows and rows of sharp fangs.

"Well, whatever it is, it looks like it's guarding *that*," Raph said, nodding to a strange domed structure anchored to the seafloor.

Raph had spotted the Kraang's underwater facility!

Inside the Turtle Sub, Leo turned back to his brothers. If they wanted to infiltrate the facility, they'd have to sneak by that giant beast.

"Let's go stealth," Leo commanded.

At nearly a hundred feet below the water, the Turtles deactivated every light on the Turtle Sub. The hull around them was cast into complete darkness.

They were swimming blind.

CHAPTER
20

While the Turtles were searching for a way into the Kraang's underwater base, April was up on the street, looking for something just as important: a nice hot meal. She also needed to take her mind off what had happened earlier. After all, it wasn't every day that a girl got exposed to a lethal alien concoction and walked away without a mark on her.

What's wrong with me? she wondered.

April hoped that a familiar face and some good food would be enough to make her feel normal again. She headed to Mr. Murakami's Noodle Shop, but she was surprised by what she found there. Outside the front door stood a strange new vending machine that was covered with buttons marked by words in a foreign language.

"What is this thing?" April wondered, inching forward for a closer look.

"Oh, that's how you order. They have these in Tokyo," a voice said from behind her.

April turned, looking up to see a punk-rock Japanese girl about her age stepping out of the shadows. She inserted a coin into the bizarre machine and pushed a button. *Clunk.* A token popped out.

"You give this to the chef," the mysterious girl told her.

"Oh, thanks," April replied. She followed the girl's instruction and made her selection.

"Mind if I join you?" the mysterious girl asked.

April paused for a moment. She was already having a strange day, so why not do something out of the ordinary and have dinner with a total stranger?

"Sure! Why not?" April said, opening the old wooden door of her favorite restaurant.

Inside, Mr. Murakami stirred a fresh, steaming hot pot of noodles. He was an excellent chef. He also happened to be blind, but that didn't slow him down for a minute.

"Hi, Murakami-*san*," April said.

Mr. Murakami recognized April's voice instantly and turned to greet her with a smile.

"April-*chan*! How are you?"

April handed Murakami her food token. He felt the round piece of wood, reading its symbols with his fingers.

"Ah, pizza *gyoza* . . . ," Murakami said.

"Hai! Chou ishi!" April answered. This was Japanese for "Yes! Delicious!"

"Oh, you speak Japanese?" the mysterious girl asked with surprise.

"I picked up a few words from—"

April paused abruptly midsentence. She was about to say "the Turtles." But knowing how weird that would sound to her new friend, she twisted the truth and finished her thought: *". . . my brothers."*

"Brothers?" the girl said. "Tell me about them."

"Oh, you know—" April stumbled, trying to think of a way to describe them that wouldn't sound like total insanity to a normal, everyday person. "They're just crazy—"

"Real animals," the mysterious girl said with a smile.

"Pretty much," April replied, giggling to herself.

"Although," the mysterious girl said, switching gears, "I never heard of pizza *gyoza* back in Tokyo."

"That's because Murakami invented it. You should try one."

"Sounds great. You should try some of mine."

"Done."

The mysterious girl handed her food token to Murakami. He flinched when he felt the order. It was a dish he didn't want to prepare.

"So, what's your name?" the mysterious girl asked.

"I'm April."

"My name's . . . Harmony."

April smiled. And "Harmony" smiled back, knowing that April had no idea who she really was.

CHAPTER 21

Under the waves of the East River, the Turtles were no closer to the Kraang's facility. But the sea monster was getting very close to them!

The creature swam up within striking distance of the Sub, licking its lips like it was looking at its dinner.

It was time for Plan B: deepwater distraction!

Donnie flipped a switch and *FLOOOOM!* He fired a high-powered flare into the depths.

As if on cue, the sea monster forgot about the Sub and swam after the twinkling light like an overactive puppy playing fetch. The coast was clear! The Turtle Sub charted a direct course for the Kraang's facility.

The Turtles saw a suction pipe begin to siphon water at an alarming rate.

"We gotta get in there before that sea monster comes back," Leo said, looking through the periscope.

Leo kept his eyes on that suction pipe and formulated a plan to sneak in.

The Turtle Sub descended to the seafloor and hovered just above a pile of rocks. Donnie manned the Sub's main controls, waiting for Leo to give him the signal. When he did, Donnie lowered the Sub's neck, opening its "mouth," which was actually an iron hatch door, and skillfully picked up one of the rocks with it.

He transported the boulder up to the Kraang's suction pipe and flung it in with a mighty swing! Moments later, it was sucked up into the water spout, jamming the pipe.

Inside, the base shook underfoot like an earthquake. Malfunction alerts lit up every screen. It was clear that something was very wrong.

"Kraang," said one droid to another, "there is a blockage which is preventing the flow of that which has been blocked."

"Kraang must come with Kraang to dislodge the blockage that needs dislodging," the other droid replied.

The droids approached a reentry pool—a small oasis in the middle of the room that was a direct doorway to the river—and jumped in.

The pair of Kraang-droids propelled themselves over to the vacuum ports and began the daunting task of unblocking the main suction pipe. They tugged and tugged, trying to loosen the rock—completely unaware that the Turtles were on the other side of the base, sneaking in.

One by one, the Turtles emerged from the base's reentry pool. They shook the water off their shells and found themselves inside a high-tech room that resembled a spaceship. Blinking lights, otherworldly machines, and alien symbols were all around them. They had made it inside the Kraang's underwater facility!

But the celebration would have to wait. Raph looked through one of the porthole windows just as a gigantic shadow passed by it—the sea monster!

"That thing is back," Raph announced. "How are we gonna get out of here?"

"We'll worry about that later," Leo decided. "Right now, we've got bigger fish to fry."

"I don't think we're gonna find a bigger fish than that," Mikey said with a smirk.

The other Turtles shot him a look, groaning loudly.

"What?" Mikey protested with a smile. "C'mon, that was good. You gotta give me that one!"

CHAPTER 22

The more they spoke, the more suspicious April became of her new friend Harmony. She couldn't put it into words. This girl she'd just met seemed to want to know an awful lot about her personal life and her friends.

Something isn't right, April noted.

The girl would have to crack eventually. *Right?*

"So, what brings you to New York?" April asked.

"I'm with my dad. He's here trying to close an old deal," Harmony answered with hesitation.

"Oh, what does he do?" April asked, covering her nerves by prepping her chopsticks casually.

Harmony paused, taking a moment to word her answer. "He's in kitchen utensils. Knives, mostly."

April logged another mental note: *Father works with knives.*

Before April could ask another question, Murakami delivered their dishes, a trail of steam following the meals all the way from the kitchen.

Harmony gave Murakami a traditional Japanese bow and said, *"Idatakimasu,"* which meant "Let's eat!"

Mental note number three, April thought, *this girl was raised in a traditional Japanese household.*

April noticed that Murakami was also impressed by Harmony's traditional ways. This girl knew her Japanese customs.

Out of respect, April mimicked her friend and paid respect to Mr. Murakami with a bow and an *"Idatakimasu"* of her own.

Harmony eyed April's dish with a strong curiosity. Pizza *gyoza?* They looked like normal dumplings to her. "All right! Let's see what these pizza pot stickers are all about." She scooped one off of April's plate and polished it off in one bite. "Best. Dumpling. *EVER!"*

"I know, right?" April said.

"Now you try mine."

Harmony slid her bowl over. It was a thick, murky liquid with something barely visible at the bottom. *Is that meat?* April wondered.

April scooped up some of the soupy broth.

It smelled salty. It smelled gross. It smelled *familiar.*

"What is it?" April asked.

"Soupon nabe," Harmony said. After a moment, she translated. "Turtle soup."

April's eyes grew wide as she put it all together. She knew exactly who this was. Her name wasn't Harmony. It was . . .

"Karai!" April gasped.

"In person," Karai grinned.

Panic hit April. Her heart was pounding. She had no time to lose. "Uh, I gotta go," she stuttered. She tried to make her way to the door, but Karai grabbed her skillfully with one swift move.

"I was thinking you'd come with me, April O'Neil. My father would love to meet you!"

April struggled to break free. "Let go of me!" she cried.

Hearing the commotion, and sensing his friend was in danger, Murakami took action. He grabbed a pot of boiling hot soup from the stove and threw it. The steaming liquid went airborne and splashed all over Karai!

"I am so sorry!" Murakami said, pretending it was an accident. He blocked Karai's path, which allowed April enough time to break free and head for the street.

April crossed to the opposite corner and took out her T-Phone to dial the Turtles.

The Turtles moved carefully through the Kraang's underwater facility, gracefully somersaulting onto the rafters overlooking the main control room. They saw a group of Kraang-droids working below.

"Okay," Leo whispered to the others, "we have to be quiet."

"Do you have to say that every time?" Donnie whispered back. "We're ninjas. We know how to be quiet."

Then, as if on cue, Donnie's T-Phone rang.

The Turtles gasped in unison, their eyes bugging out at the Kraang-droids, who were now staring right at them.

"Ooh, that is embarrassing!" Mikey said with a chuckle.

The army of droids picked up their blasters and opened fire, unleashing a barrage of energy bolts that scorched holes in the wall behind the Turtles. The ninjas scattered.

Donnie cartwheeled for cover and answered his T-Phone. It was April.

"April, hi, it's *not* a great time!" Donnie said, barely dodging a hail of laser blasts.

"Donnie! Karai's after me!" he heard April say.

"What?!" Donnie shouted over the sound of ricocheting blasts. "I'm sorry," he told her, trying to sound cool and composed. "We can't get there. But don't worry. Stay calm!" And then, in a sudden, frantic voice, he added, "And run! Run for your life!"

CHAPTER 24

Don't stop.

That was what April told herself as she hung up her T-Phone and sprinted toward a crowd on the street. After turning a corner, she looked back and gasped. Karai was right there, in hot pursuit!

April panted. She was getting tired. She needed a set of wheels! Up ahead on the street, she saw her chance: a pizza guy was getting off his moped to make a delivery—

April knew what she had to do.

"Hey!" she called out to the pizza guy, distracting him. "Is that pizza for April O'Neil?"

"No," the pizza guy said, looking down to check his delivery label. "It's for—"

But before he could finish, he saw April steal his moped and take off! "Hey! What are you doing?!" he yelled.

"I'll bring it back! I promise!" April shouted over the engine. She knew she shouldn't have stolen that guy's ride, but this was a life-or-death situation. *I'll make it up to him,* she swore to herself.

Karai caught up to the pizza guy, who was yelling about a girl who'd just stolen his moped. The corners of her mouth turned up in a smile. She relished a good chase as much as the next ninja. If her opponent wanted a high-speed race, she'd get one!

Karai disappeared into a darkened alley and hopped aboard her Dragon Chopper, which had been stashed behind a Dumpster. She strapped on her helmet and kick started her sleek motorcycle, gunning the engine. She peeled out, a curlicue of tire tracks in her wake, nearly running over the pizza guy as she sped onto the street. With this kind of horse-power, she'd catch up to April in no time!

A few blocks ahead, April hit a traffic light. She checked her rearview mirror. No sign of Karai. She breathed easy for a second, thinking she'd lost her, when—

Something made a deafening screech right behind her. She turned to see the Dragon Chop-per hopping over a taxicab at high speed. Karai was closing in!

April was shaking. She released the brake and ran the red light. Horns blared as she cut off an oncoming truck, nearly causing a three-car pileup. She was so scared that she didn't see Karai's Dragon Chopper gaining on her, tracking her moped's every move.

Karai revved up alongside her, swinging at her with her fist. She couldn't connect, so she sideswiped April with the front of the Chopper, bumping April's moped onto a crowded sidewalk. April maneuvered through an obstacle course of fruit stands, hot dog carts, and pedestrians.

As April held on for dear life, she saw a wall up ahead. It got closer and closer. Bigger and bigger.

She jackknifed the moped, stopping inches before she would have crashed. Then she hit the gas, slingshotting the moped onto a side street.

That was a close one, April thought as she heard the asphalt crack behind her. She checked the rearview again—

It was Karai! Her Chopper's front tire had come down in a hard landing. She was still in hot pursuit.

Ahead of April a big delivery truck was slowly backing down the cross street, almost blocking traffic completely. She'd be stopped cold in a moment, and if that happened, she'd be doomed.

But there was a narrow gap between the truck and the corner of a wall. It was barely a foot across—and shrinking with each moment.

Luckily, she was driving the smallest moped on the market. She revved the engine. The needle on the speedometer vibrated at top speed.

This moped might barely be able to get through, she thought. *If only I can get there in time—*

April's adrenaline kicked into overdrive.

Don't stop, she told herself. *Don't stop.* She gunned the engine, held her breath, and hoped for the best—

She did it! Keeping the moped steady, she made it around the truck before it blocked the street completely. She had made it to safety, leaving Karai in the dust.

CHAPTER 25

At that very moment, as his brothers were caught in a firefight with a squad of Kraang-droids, Donnie was trying to call April back on his T-Phone. He was in a total state of worry, oblivious to the blaster fire that whizzed all around him. Leo attempted to reason with him in a firm but calm tone. "Donnie, focus! April can take care of herself."

"Against Karai?" Donnie asked in a frenzy. April barely knew how to throw a punch, and Karai had nearly taken out a Kraang spaceship *on her own*! "Are you kidding? I've gotta help her!"

"You're not gonna be much help if you get blasted in the head!" Leo yelled.

"Whoa!" Donnie shouted, ducking an energy

bolt that nearly scorched his scalp. "Good point!"

Time to get my shell in the game! Donnie thought, charging into battle with his brothers.

Leo broke through the Kraang first, his *kata-nas* slicing and dicing through two droids at once. Donnie was right behind him, unleashing his *bo* staff at the last second for a surprise attack. The backup bots never knew what hit them. And just as two remaining Kraang-droids were about to open fire, their titanium bodies hit the floor, thanks to Mikey's sweet sweeper kick.

"That's a twofer!" Mikey bragged, gratefully bowing to an imaginary crowd like a rock star finishing a sold-out performance. "Thank you. And thank you. And thank you."

Two Kraang-droids suddenly appeared behind Mikey, readying their blasters, and Raph rushed into action. He vaulted himself into the air, surprising the bots with a nose dive–style *sai* strike. He skewered them to the floor before they could squeeze a trigger. They were nothing but scrap metal now.

"How many times have I told you no celebrating until the fight is over?!" Raph scolded Mikey.

"How many times have I told *you* I assumed it was over?" Mikey retorted, jabbing Raph with his finger. Raph grabbed Mikey's hand and squeezed. Hard.

Mikey screamed.

Donnie couldn't believe this! Were they really having an argument *now*? He got between them before it got any worse. "Children! Children! We have got to go."

"Um, have you forgotten about a little something called completing the mission?" Leo said, reminding them all why they were standing in the middle of an underwater base in the first place.

"But April's in danger!" Donnie insisted.

"If we leave now, the Kraang will poison everyone in New York," Raph reminded him. "Which, last time, I checked, includes April!"

"Think, Donnie! How do we take this place out?" Leo asked.

Donnie scanned the control room around

them, trying to concentrate on finding a solution. How were they going to destroy this facility? He needed a hint, a sign of some kind.

"The chemical is highly explosive," Donnie said.

"How do you know that?" Mikey asked.

"Partly because it has hydrocarbon on its outer ring," he explained. "And partly because of that sign," he added, pointing at a picture on the wall.

They all looked up. There was a warning diagram showing a Kraang exploding out of a droid body.

Donnie swiped a blaster from one of the bots lying motionless on the floor. "Raph, you think you can get this blaster open for me?"

Raph spun one *sai* with a wicked smile. "With pleasure."

"But before you do, be careful you don't—"

Before Donnie could finish, Raph stabbed the weapon, peeling off half its metal casing with one swipe. Donnie winced and shut his eyes. He nervously peeked a moment later.

"Oh, good, we're still alive," he said with a

sigh. He fiddled with the blaster's wiring. "Now I'll short out the power supply and leave it by the chemical tanks. It'll overheat and the whole place will go boom."

Once the blaster was ready to detonate, Donnie and the other Turtles got into position. Leo and Raph ran across the room, directly under the chemical tanks, which were mounted to the ceiling. If Donnie was going to plant the explosive up there, he was going to need a boost.

So, like gymnasts prepping for a routine, Leo and Raph locked arms, forming a launching pad. Donnie sprinted toward them, vaulted off their arms, and propelled himself through the air. He arced over the room, getting some serious hang time, and planted the blaster perfectly.

"There," Donnie said as he dropped to the ground. "In about ninety seconds, this whole place is gonna blow."

Satisfied that their mission was nearly complete, Leo gave the go-ahead. "All right! Let's move!"

Donnie redialed April on his T-Phone. He heard her panting when she picked up. "April, what's your status?"

"Could . . . be . . . better!" he heard April yell.

"Okay, we're on our way," he assured her. "We'll be there soon."

The Turtles ran back to the only exit in the entire facility: the reentry pool. All they had to do was jump in, swim back to the Sub, and they'd be home free.

But something was wrong. The water was rumbling. Something big was coming through the watery portal. A long, snakelike neck emerged from the pool. Towering over the Turtles was a scaly amphibian beast with rows of sharp fangs.

It was the sea monster!

"Uh, actually, there might be a slight delay," Donnie said into the T-Phone.

They were trapped!

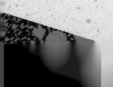

CHAPTER 26

The Turtles darted around the room, desperately trying to dodge the sea monster.

The creature roared, thrashing its head around the facility like a monstrous wrecking ball.

How can things get any worse? Leo wondered, watching the sea monster almost eat Raph like a snack.

As if on cue, Donnie seemed to answer that unasked question. "We've only got thirty seconds before that blaster explodes!"

"Uh, guys, any ideas?" Leo asked.

"Let's see," Donnie began. "We're cornered by an amphibious sea monster in an underwater base that's about to blow up." Donnie paused for a

second, then threw in the towel. "I'm out!"

Time seemed to slow as Leo watched the beast smack Raph down like a rag doll, its tentacle-like neck taking Donnie off his feet in the process. Leo felt like there was nothing he could do. He wasn't going to be able to bail his bros out of this battle.

But just as Leo was about to give up all hope, he heard an earsplitting war cry. He turned to see Mikey jumping into action.

Mikey unleashed the chain from his *nunchucks,* swinging it around the sea monster's snout. The beast reared its terrible head, pulling the chain forward. Mikey hung on for the wildest ride of his life!

Leo joined Raph and Donnie as they cheered Mikey. He was like a rodeo rider, using all his strength and balance to stay on top of the creature and fight its wild bucking like a pro.

Mikey sat on its head, enjoying a bird's-eye view of the room. And even though he was being jostled like crazy, he spotted a tiny lever.

Mikey had a feeling it was important.

He took a deep breath and jumped. In one fluid motion, he caught the lever, switched it off, and tumbled to the ground. The reentry pool doors slammed shut, snaring the sea monster in a giant steel trap!

"Woo-hoo! That was fun!" Mikey exclaimed, breaking into another victory dance.

"Mikey! That dance better not last more than four seconds!" Donnie shouted.

Mikey grooved for three seconds, then used that final second to somersault after his bros and swim out to safety toward the Sub.

The Kraang underwater base vibrated uncontrollably and finally exploded, sending a shockwave through the water that was so strong, it thrust the Turtles through the Sub's hatch.

Behind them, the facility crumbled to the seafloor, kicking up an aquatic sand cloud that blanketed the destruction in a watery, milky fog. After a few moments, the depths of the river cleared, leaving the fish and the seaweed around it unharmed.

New York City's water supply was safe . . . for now.

Inside the cockpit of the Turtle Sub, Raph confidently remarked, "Hey, that wasn't such a chore, now was it?"

Donnie brought the navigation systems up online. "Great," he said with relief. "Now we can get back to April and— Oh no. Are you kidding me?!"

They all went to the Sub's porthole to look out. A massive figure swam rapidly toward them.

The sea monster. The Sub looked like a bath toy compared to the enormous beast.

Inside, watching the monster through the periscope, Leo pleaded with Donnie. "Can you make this thing go faster?"

"Of course I can," Donnie said, pressing a button. The Sub's emergency booster rockets roared to life—and flew away on their own, zipping through the East River like runaway torpedoes.

They weren't properly attached!

The Sub floated silently. It was completely defenseless against the monster.

"Wow, that is fast!" Mikey said, watching the engines disappear into the distance.

"Pedal! Faster!" Donnie frantically shouted.

Leo, Raph, and Mikey snapped back to the moment and hit the stationary bikes once more. They were exhausted, and in no condition to pedal their way to safety, but they had no choice.

"Feelin' the burn!" Mikey said, pedaling furiously.

Just then, the Turtle Sub creaked loudly. And kept creaking. Almost like something was crushing it like a tin can. The walls closed in.

The sea monster had the Sub in its grasp, its long tail and flippers enveloping the craft completely. It squeezed harder.

"That's it! It's got us! We're all gonna die!" Donnie screamed.

The Turtles braced themselves for implosion, locking their eyes shut and listening to the strained sounds of the Sub caving under the pressure.

Then everything stopped.

The creaking sounds ceased, giving way to a different kind of noise altogether—a strange, guttural animal noise the Turtles had never heard before. They weren't scary sounds. They were almost soothing. A musical animal call never heard on planet Earth before.

Raph turned to his brothers and let out a disgusted noise of his own. Leo felt the pressure loosen up on the walls and realized that the monster wasn't squashing the Sub.

It was hugging it.

"I think it's in love," Leo said.

"Hey!" Mikey protested, grossed out. "We're not that kind of Sub!"

Donnie saw his chance. He pulled a lever, releasing small stun-mines from the Sub's weapon hatches. The explosives detonated, scaring the beast away from its submarine soul mate.

Mikey felt a little bad that the Turtles had to break the monster's heart. But as they pedaled the Sub away, he knew the sea monster wouldn't be sad for long. After all, there were plenty of fish in the sea.

CHAPTER 27

Karai's Dragon Chopper screeched to a stop. She cut the engine and investigated a few back alleys on foot. It was only a matter of time before she found April and brought her back to Shredder like a trophy.

Suddenly, April sprang up behind her, swinging the pizza guy's bike helmet like a weapon.

"You've got guts," Karai admitted, evading April's attack. "Let's see if I can pound that out of you."

April stood her ground. She locked eyes with Karai, snapping a strange-looking fan out of her purse.

"A *tessen,*" Karai said, impressed by April's

weapon of choice. It looked like an ordinary fan, but it was actually made of metal and wood—and was sharp enough to cut through steel. "It's beautiful and unassuming, but very powerful . . . in the right hands."

April lunged forward, using the *tessen* like a sword. She sliced through the air furiously. Karai used her ninja know-how and lightning-fast reflexes to reverse April's move and swipe the *tessen* away. Karai threw it to the ground, taunting her.

Karai opened up her stance, and April attacked. She thought back to the *katas* that Master Splinter had taught her: power-punching in set patterns. She fought hard, determined to land a hit on Karai, who dodged the strikes gracefully.

This is too easy, Karai thought, just as she felt the wind get knocked out of her and an insane pain shoot through her torso. April had landed a kick!

Karai was stunned. It wasn't often that someone surprised her in battle. She doubled over. "Good one."

"Glad you enjoyed it." April scowled.

"Now it's my turn."

Karai made short work of April, pummeling her blow by blow. With every hit, it became more and more difficult for April to pick herself up again. And with a combo of punches and kicks, Karai knocked April clear out of the alley and onto the busy sidewalk.

"What makes you so special?" Karai said bitterly. "You're the center of an alien conspiracy, protected by mutants, and trained by a great ninja master. Why?"

"I don't know." April winced, staggering back up on her feet. Then, in a burst of rage, she grabbed Karai in a wrestling hold. The two girls grappled, unaware that they were inching closer to the subway entrance.

"I'm flunking trig, my friends are mutants, aliens got my dad, and I lost my mother!" April yelled.

Karai froze, abruptly letting go of April. "You lost your mother, too?" she asked with a tremble in her voice, backing off.

Splinter's teachings echoed through April's mind: *The key is to unbalance your opponent.*

Noticing they were at the top of the subway stairwell, April saw her opportunity to unbalance Karai. She used her opponent's moment of hesitation to deliver a hard kick. Karai tumbled down the stairs and vanished into the shadows of the subway.

In that moment, a whole new April stood up. Gone was the damsel in distress. The girl who stood at the top of those stairs was a true *kunoichi* now. Exhausted and bruised but triumphant!

April smiled. "Not bad for a nobody."

CHAPTER 28

The moment the Turtles docked the Sub outside the lair, Donnie dialed April on his T-Phone. With every unanswered ring, he became more anxious.

"Come on, April, come on, April . . ."

"Hey, Donnie!" he heard her voice say over the speaker.

Instant relief washed over him. "April! You're okay!" He was so overjoyed that he yelled it through the sewers at the top of his lungs. "You hear that, guys? My sweet princess is alive!"

And with that, Donnie's face turned bright red. "Did I mute that?" he asked her.

"Let's just agree that you did," April replied.

Normally, that would have mortified Donnie. But not today. His not-so-secret crush was coming home! He smiled. "You got it!"

A short while later, the Turtles and Master Splinter were gathered around April, listening to her recount her fight with Karai. "When her guard was down, I flipped her down the subway steps and bolted!"

Amazed by her story, and proud of her bravery, each of the Turtles cheered her on in their own way.

"That is awesome!" Donnie said, beaming.

"You rock!" Mikey complimented her.

"Kick-butt!" Raph agreed.

"Impressive, April. You used your training well," Master Splinter said. "And you fulfilled the most important goal of the ninja—to come home alive."

"Thank you, Sensei." April bowed. "Looks like I can take care of myself after all."

"Yes. And no."

April gave her master a puzzled look. He was obviously proud of her, but his solemn tone indicated he was about to give her some bad news.

"Karai may have failed this time," Splinter told her. "But if Shredder wants you, he will stop at nothing to find you. And with the Kraang after you as well, the wisest decision is for you to remain here, in the sewer, with us."

April's eyes widened. "What?!"

"That's great!" Donnie blurted out—until he looked up at an obviously devastated April. He masked his excitement and mumbled, "I mean, that's horrible . . . that your life as you know it is over . . . and I'll shut up now."

"I can't stay down here!" April protested. "I mean, what about school? My friends? Everything?!"

"April, Master Splinter's right," Leo said, trying to reason with her. "Until we stop Shredder and the Kraang, this is the only place you're safe."

April stared down at the floor, deep in thought. *Am I really about to give up my normal life?*

She looked around the room at the faces of the mutants who wanted to help her. With her dad out of the picture, they were the closest thing she had to a family.

"So once we stop them, I can have my life back?" April asked.

"Yes," Leo replied.

And with that, April made up her mind. She looked up at Master Splinter and the others with confidence—that same confidence she had gained when she had bested Karai. If she could do that, she could do anything.

Her eyes narrowed. She was ready for whatever challenges were ahead of her.

"Let's get started."